For BooBoo

This is BooBoo.

BooBoo is a gosling.

A small, blue gosling
who likes to eat.

BooBoo likes to eat from
morning till night.

Every day.

In the morning she eats
everything in her food bowl.

"Good food," she says.

BooBoo visits the hens
and gobbles their grain.

"Good food," she says.

BooBoo visits the goat
and pokes her beak into the trough.

"Good food," she says.

BooBoo visits the mouse
and nibbles from his dish.

"Good food," she says.

Every afternoon BooBoo
goes for a swim in the pond.

She tastes the weeds.
"Good food," she says.

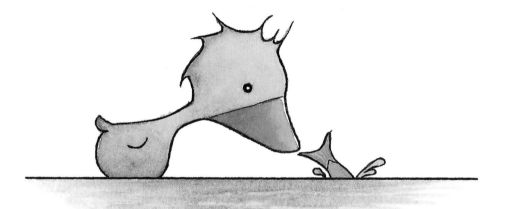

BooBoo is a curious, blue gosling.

Who likes to eat.

One afternoon BooBoo saw bubbles
floating over the pond.

She opened her beak and swallowed
a bright blue bubble.

"Good food," said BooBoo.

Then she burped.

She burped forwards.

She burped backwards.

She burped under water.

She burped in the weeds.

"Drink water!" said the turtle.
BooBoo guzzled and gulped water.

She burped a teeny tiny bubble.
"Good food," she said.

BooBoo is a gosling.
A small, blue gosling who likes to eat.
Almost everything!

First published in Great Britain 2005 by Walker Books Ltd
87 Vauxhall Walk, London SE11 5HJ

This edition published 2006

2 4 6 8 10 9 7 5 3 1

© 2004 Olivier Dunrea
Published by arrangement with Houghton Mifflin Company

This book has been typeset in Shannon

Printed in China

All rights reserved

British Library Cataloguing in Publication Data:
a catalogue record for this book is available from the British Library

ISBN-13: 978-1-4063-0139-7
ISBN-10: 1-4063-0139-6

www.walkerbooks.co.uk

BooBoo

Olivier Dunrea